Stolen Ponies

Do you love ponies? Be a Pony Pal!

Look for these Pony Pal books:

#1 I Want a Pony
#2 A Pony for Keeps
#3 A Pony in Trouble
#4 Give Me Back My Pony
#5 Pony to the Rescue
#6 Too Many Ponies
#7 Runaway Pony
#8 Good-bye Pony
#9 The Wild Pony
Super Special #1 The Baby Pony
#10 Don't Hurt My Pony
#11 Circus Pony
#12 Keep Out, Pony!
#13 The Girl Who Hated Ponies
#14 Pony-Sitters
Super Special #2 The Story of Our Ponies
#15 The Blind Pony
#16 The Missing Pony Pal
#17 Detective Pony
#18 The Saddest Pony
#19 Moving Pony

coming soon

#21 The Winning Pony

Stolen Ponies

Jeanne Betancourt

illustrated by Vivien Kubbos

SCHOLASTIC
SYDNEY AUCKLAND NEW YORK TORONTO LONDON MEXICO CITY
NEW DELHI HONG KONG BUENOS AIRES PUERTO RICO

Scholastic Australia Pty Limited
PO Box 579, Gosford NSW 2250
ABN 11 000 614 577
www.scholastic.com.au

Part of the Scholastic Group
Sydney • Auckland • New York • Toronto • London • Mexico City
• New Delhi • Hong Kong • Buenos Aires • Puerto Rico

First published by Scholastic Australia in 1998.
This edition published by Scholastic Australia in 2007.

Illustrations by Vivien Kubbos.

ISBN 978-1-74169-054-5

Printed by McPherson's Printing Group, Victoria.

10 9 8 7 6 5 4 3 2 8 9 / 0

Contents

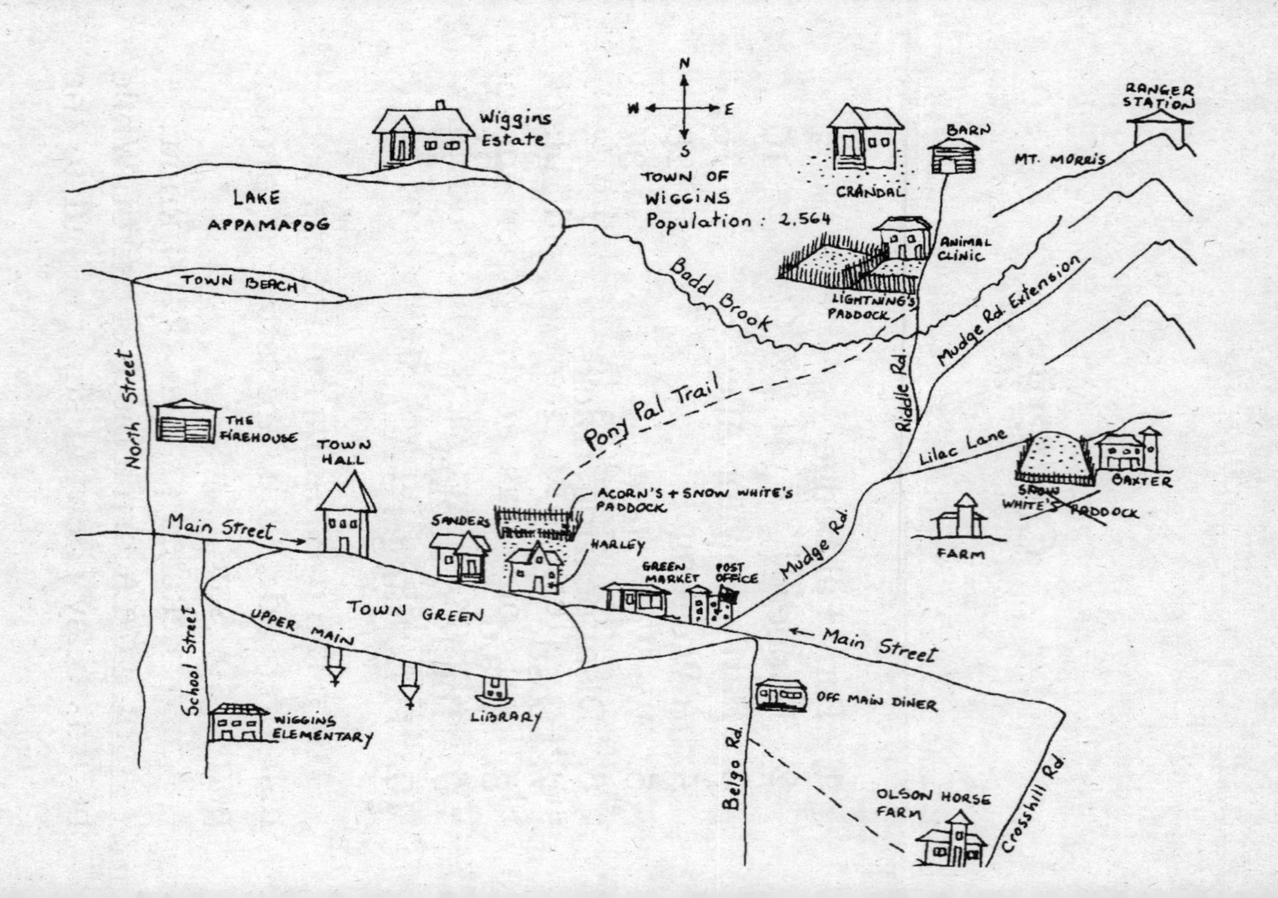

N
W
E
S
TOWN OF
WIGGINS
Population : 2,564
Wiggins
Estate
LAKE
APPAMAPOG
TOWN BEACH
CRANDAL
BARN
RANGER
STATION
MT. MORRIS
ANIMAL
CLINIC
LIGHTNING'S
PADDOCK
Badd Brook
Mudge Rd. Extension
Riddle Rd.
Pony Pal Trail
North Street
THE
FIREHOUSE
TOWN
HALL
Main Street
SANDERS
ACORN'S + SNOW WHITE'S
PADDOCK
HARLEY
GREEN
MARKET
POST
OFFICE
Mudge Rd.
Lilac Lane
SNOW
WHITE'S
PADDOCK
BAXTER
FARM
TOWN GREEN
UPPER MAIN
School Street
WIGGINS
ELEMENTARY
LIBRARY
Main Street
OFF MAIN DINER
Belgo Rd.
OLSON HORSE
FARM
Crosshill Rd.

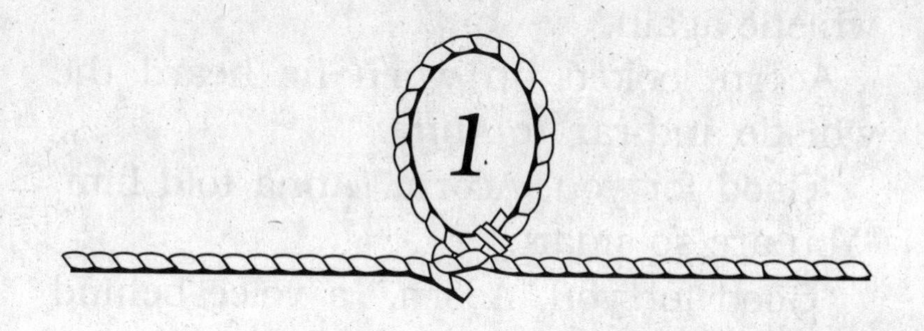

Pony Pal Lodge

Anna Harley stood in front of the pony shelter. Her cute brown and black Shetland pony was at the other end of the paddock. Anna blew one loud blast on her whistle and yelled, "Acorn, come on."

Acorn ran over. Anna smiled and patted his forehead. "You are such a perfect pony," she said.

Acorn nickered as if to say, "I know."

Anna gave Acorn a piece of carrot. While he was busy chewing she ran out to the middle of the paddock. Anna blew her whistle again.

Acorn looked up when he heard the whistle and ran to Anna.

"Good for you, Acorn," Anna told him. "You are so smart."

"Good for you, Acorn," a voice behind Anna repeated in a sing-song voice. "You are so smart."

Anna swung around and faced Tommy Rand and Mike Lacey. The boys were leaning on the paddock fence with their bikes. Anna didn't like Tommy and Mike. They were eighth graders who thought they were big deals and they were always annoying Anna and her Pony Pals.

"You guys," Anna exclaimed, "get off my property!"

"You guys," Tommy and Mike repeated in unison, "get off my property!"

"I mean it," shouted Anna.

"I mean it," the boys repeated.

Anna noticed her Pony Pal, Lulu,

silently running up behind Tommy and Mike. Tommy and Mike didn't see Lulu.

Anna put her hands on her hips. "Don't you two have anything better to do with your time?" she asked.

"Oh, she's getting angry," Tommy said with a laugh.

When Lulu was right behind the boys, she put her whistle to her lips and blew. The sudden, shrill sound startled Mike and Tommy, and they both jumped.

"Sorry," Lulu said. "Did I scare you?"

"NO!" Tommy lied.

"'Course not," added Mike.

"NO!" mimicked Anna. "'Course not."

"The Pony Pests are too stupid," said Tommy.

"Let's go," Mike said.

Tommy and Mike hopped onto their trail bikes.

"Good riddance," said Lulu.

"When are the pests going to grow up and get real horses?" Tommy asked Mike.

"They're too afraid of real horses," sneered Mike.

The boys jerked their bikes up on the rear wheels, brought the front wheels down, and pedaled away.

"You're the pests, you gonzos," Anna yelled after them.

Lulu put her hand on Anna's arm. "Forget about them," she said. "They're not worth the trouble."

"You're right," Anna agreed.

"Let's go to our new hideout," said Lulu. "Those guys can't bother us at Pony Pal Lodge."

The girls packed their saddle bags with supplies for their new hideout and saddled up Acorn and Snow White.

As Anna swung into the saddle she thought, I don't care what Tommy and Mike say. I don't need a horse. I love my pony and I'm going to ride Acorn forever. He's perfect for me.

Anna and Lulu rode onto Pony Pal Trail. The mile-and-a-half trail through the

woods led to Pam Crandal's place. Pam and her pony, Lightning, were there waiting for Anna and Lulu in the Crandals' big field at the end of the trail.

The Pony Pals pulled their ponies into a circle.

"Did you bring everything?" asked Pam.

"I've got a hammer and nails," said Anna. "The nails are big enough to make the hitching post. And I brought some drawings of ponies to put on the walls."

"Great," said Pam. She patted the red pail hanging off the back of her saddle. "I've brought this for watering our ponies, and a tin of oats. I also found an old curry comb and brush in the barn that we can leave in the hideout."

"I've got a book to help us identify birds and mammals," said Lulu. "And a big flashlight."

"Lulu and I made a map of how to get to our hideout," Anna told Pam.

"Show her," said Lulu.

Anna reached into her saddle bag and

pulled out a piece of folded drawing paper and showed it to Pam.

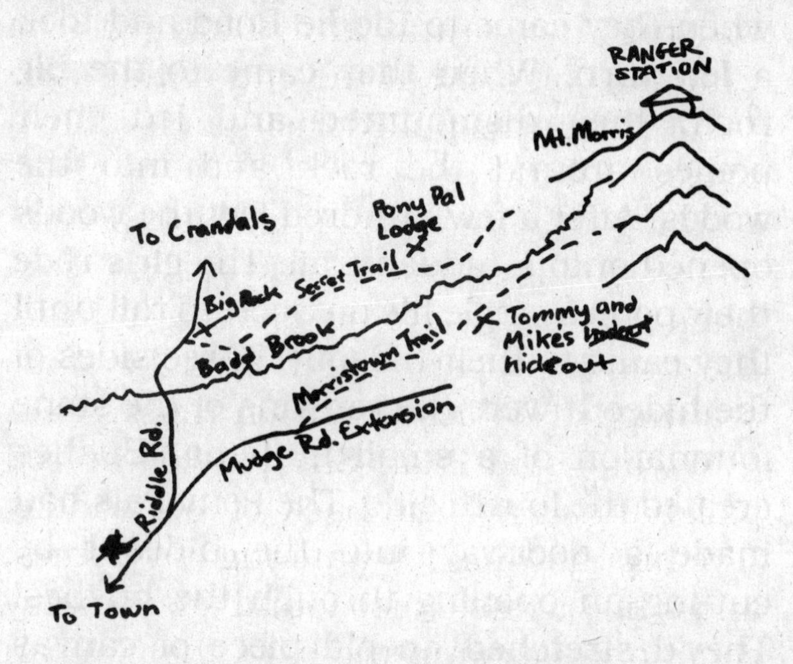

"We call the trail we found behind the big rock, Secret Trail," explained Anna.

"That's perfect," said Pam.

"Let's put dry pine needles on the floor of our hideout," suggested Lulu.

"That would look pretty," said Anna.

"It would smell good, too," said Pam. She turned Lightning around. "Let's go."

The Pony Pals galloped across the Crandals' big field. They slowed down when they came to Riddle Road and took a left turn. When they came to the big rock, they dismounted and led their ponies around the rock and into the woods. After a few hundred feet the woods opened onto a hidden trail. The girls rode their ponies single file on Secret Trail until they came to their hideout. Three sides of the hideout were the remains of the stone foundation of a small building. Bushes created the fourth side. The Pony Pals had made a doorway into the hideout by cutting an opening through the bushes. They'd stretched an old piece of canvas over the top for a roof.

"Let's make the hitching post right away," suggested Lulu. "Then we can use it."

As soon as the hitching post was ready and their ponies were tied to it, the girls set to work on the lodge. Pam made a shelf in the rock wall for their supplies. Lulu and Anna gathered pine needles and spread them out on the floor. Finally, they sat in a circle inside the hideout and had their lunch.

"After we eat let's go for a trail ride on the other side of Badd Brook," suggested Anna. "We can explore, then come back to our hideout."

Pam and Lulu agreed.

"I love that we have a secret hideout," said Lulu.

"Me, too," said Pam.

"Me, three," added Anna. "I hope nobody ever knows it's here but us."

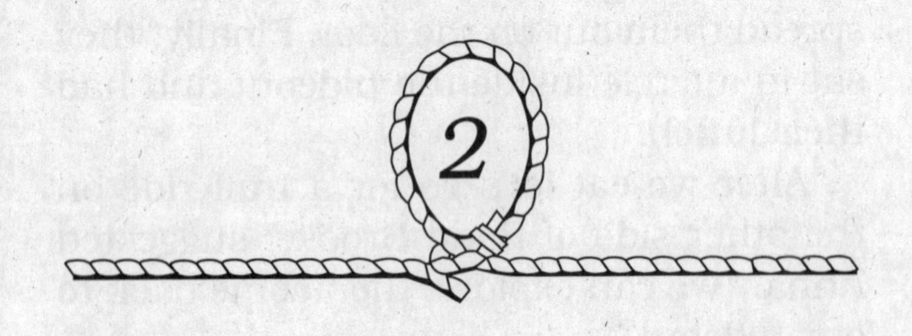

Danger!

The Pony Pals packed up their lunch wrappers and returned to their ponies. Soon they were on the trail leading to Badd Brook. There had been a lot of rain and the brook was high. But they found a safe place to ride their ponies across. Pam led the way.

As Anna followed Pam across the brook, she thought about the Pony Pals. Pam Crandal had been around horses and ponies all her life. Her mother was a riding teacher and her father was a veterinarian.

Anna and Pam had been in school together since kindergarten. Pam loved school and always got the best grades.

Anna didn't like school nearly as much as Pam. She was dyslexic, so reading, spelling, and maths were difficult for her. But Anna was a terrific artist. She loved to draw and paint, especially pictures of ponies. And she loved to be outdoors with nature.

Lulu Sanders knew the most about nature. Her father was a naturalist who traveled all over the world studying wild animals. Lulu's mother died when she was little. So Lulu had traveled everywhere with her dad. She learnt a lot about nature and animals from him.

When Lulu turned ten, her father decided that she should live with her Grandmother Sanders in Wiggins. Mrs. Sanders's house was right next door to Anna's house. At first, Lulu thought living in Wiggins would be boring. But that was before she met Anna and Pam. Now she loved living in Wiggins. The adventures she had with her Pony Pals were as exciting as the adventures she'd had traveling with her dad. And best of all, in Wiggins she could have a pony.

The Pony Pals reached the other side of the wide brook. "There's a trail over here," Pam told Anna and Lulu. They entered the narrow trail and headed into the dark woods.

They were on the trail for only a few minutes when Acorn stopped suddenly. "What's wrong, Acorn?" Anna asked.

Acorn sniffed the air and nickered fearfully.

Lulu and Pam pulled their ponies up behind Anna and Acorn. "Acorn smells something," Anna told them.

The three girls sniffed the air.

"Smoke," said Lulu. "Maybe someone has a campfire."

"Campfires aren't allowed around here," said Pam.

"Maybe it's a forest fire," said Anna with alarm.

Lulu pointed towards the woods to their left. "The smoke is coming from that direction," she said.

"We have to find that fire and try to put it out," said Pam.

The Pony Pals jumped off their ponies and led them in the direction of the smoky smell.

In a few minutes they came to a small clearing in the woods. Flames spat out of a small woodpile in the center of the clearing.

Pam called out, "Hello!"

No one answered.

"Whoever lit this campfire left it burning," said Lulu. "A little breeze could make it spread."

Pam got a water bottle from her saddle bag. She and Lulu ran over to the fire while Anna stayed with their ponies. Pam poured water on the flames. Lulu scooped

up handfuls of earth and dropped the dirt over the hot embers.

"Boy, it's lucky we found this fire," observed Lulu. "It could have really spread."

"I wonder who lit it," said Pam.

"Let's try to figure that out," suggested Lulu. "Throw some more dirt on it while I look for clues."

Lulu searched carefully around the clearing. "Here's a shoe print," she shouted. "It looks like a sneaker. Can you draw it, Anna?"

Pam held the ponies while Anna went over to Lulu and studied the clear print in the dirt. She took a small art pad and pencil from her pocket. "It will be easy to draw," she told Lulu. "Let's measure it, too."

Lulu put her right foot next to the sneaker imprint. The print was bigger than Lulu's shoe.

"How long is your pad?" she asked Anna.

"Four inches," answered Anna.

"Use it as a ruler to see how much bigger this print is than my shoe," suggested Lulu.

Anna bent over and measured. "It's about two inches longer than your boot," observed Anna.

"That's what I thought," said Lulu.

"There's a candy wrapper bag over here," shouted Pam.

Lulu went to see the candy wrapper, while Anna did a drawing of the big sneaker imprint.

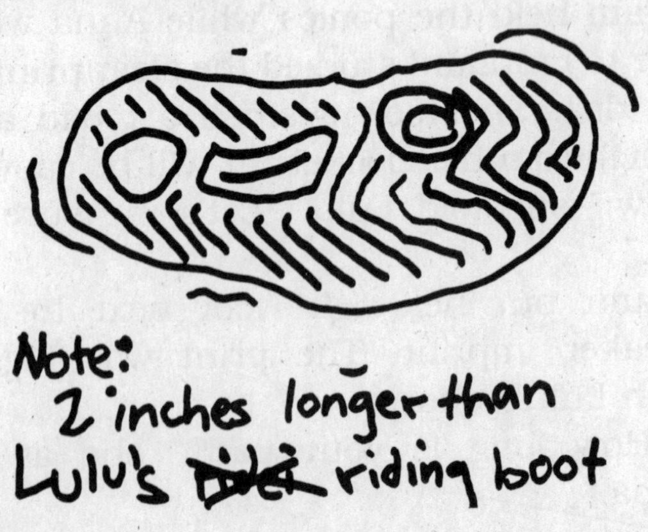

"There are more of those tracks over here," yelled Lulu. "And one that looks like a different pattern. It's not very clear."

"That means there were at least two people responsible for the fire," said Pam.

"Are there enough tracks to follow?" asked Anna.

"The Morristown Trail is over here," said Lulu. "I bet they went that way."

"They're probably campers," said Pam.

"Let's try to follow them," suggested Lulu.

"And tell them that their fire flamed up after they left it," said Pam.

What if they don't listen to us? wondered Anna. What if they don't care? What will we do then?

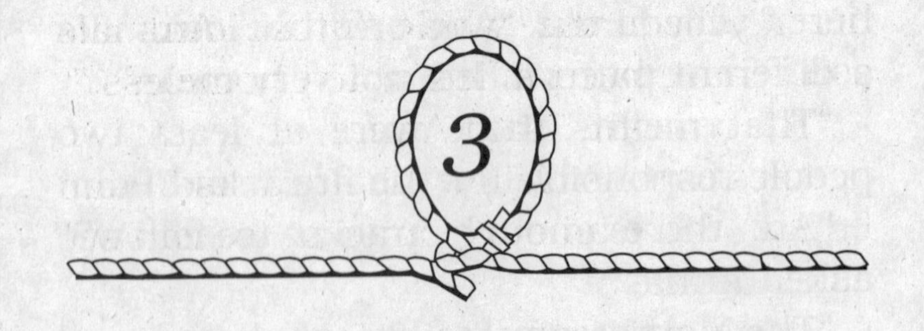

Bart's Bowling Alley

"They might not pay attention to us because we're kids," said Anna. "They might go on lighting fires."

"We'll tell them it's illegal to have campfires in the state forest," said Pam.

"If they look scary I don't want to tell them anything," said Anna.

"We'll spy on them first," said Lulu. "If they look mean or scary we won't talk to them at all. Okay?"

"Okay," agreed Anna.

"But then we should tell the Park

Ranger," said Pam. "That fire could have burnt down the whole forest. Animals could have been killed or left homeless."

"You're right," said Anna.

"Let's try to follow the tracks," said Lulu. "We'll lead our ponies so we can see clues better."

"Don't make any noise," Anna warned. "We want to find them without them seeing us."

After a few minutes on the Morristown Trail, Anna noticed a sneaker track in a muddy patch. She compared it to her drawing. They were identical.

A little farther on, Lulu put up her hand as a signal for everyone to stop. She handed Snow White's reins to Anna. "Wait here," she whispered. "I think I see something in the woods.

Lulu walked a few feet into the woods, bent over to pick something up, and came back. She held up part of a candy wrapper. It was like the wrapper that Pam had found near the campfire. Pam held the two pieces side by side. They fitted together like a puzzle.

"They definitely went into the woods here," observed Lulu.

"I'll stay with the ponies," suggested Pam. "You two go look."

"We'll be right back," Anna told Pam as she handed her Snow White's and Acorn's reins.

Lulu took her binoculars out of her saddle bag and hung them around her neck. The two girls walked into the woods and followed a deer run until it opened onto a small clearing. They hid behind a honeysuckle bush and Lulu peered through her binoculars.

"Do you see anyone?" Anna whispered.

"No," said Lulu. "But someone's been here."

Lulu handed the binoculars to Anna. "Look towards that hole in the rock ledge," she told her. Anna pointed the binoculars to an opening at the base of the ledge. She

saw the remains of a campfire in front of the opening.

"That fire isn't smoking," said Anna.

"Maybe they made this fire another day," said Lulu. "They might hang out in these woods, too. I bet that cave is their hideout."

"Let's go see," suggested Lulu.

"What if they're in there?" asked Anna.

"We'll sneak around from the other side of the rock ledge," said Lulu. "Maybe we'll hear voices if they are in there."

Lulu and Anna moved cautiously through the woods to the rock ledge. Then they crept along the rock until they were beside the opening.

Anna held her breath and listened. She didn't hear any voices.

She leant over and peeked into the cave. No one was in there. But she did see the remains of another fire. Also, some scattered soda cans, a crunched-up paper bag, and a big stick leaning against the rock wall.

She motioned to Lulu with her arm. "Come on."

Anna and Lulu went into the cave.

"What a mess," said Lulu. "Look." Lulu was pointing at ashes that had blown from the fire onto the floor. A sneaker print was clearly outlined in the ashes.

Anna pulled out her drawing pad from her pocket and compared the print to her drawing. "It was made by the same shoe," she told Lulu.

"And here's another clue," said Lulu. She picked up a book of matches and read out loud, "Bart's Bowling Alley."

"There isn't any place like that around here," said Anna.

"It also says, 'Chicago's best bowling'," added Lulu.

"Chicago," repeated Anna. "Do you think they're campers who came all the way from Chicago?"

"Or they could have visited Chicago," suggested Lulu.

"Mike Lacey's father lives in Chicago!"

exclaimed Anna. "Mike just came back from visiting him."

Anna held up an empty root beer can. "Tommy Rand loves root beer," she said. Ants swarmed out of the can. She dropped it.

Lulu put her finger to her lips. "Listen," she whispered. Anna heard a whistle blast.

"It's Pam," said Anna. "She's warning us."

Anna and Lulu ran out of the cave and back through the woods towards the trail. Anna's heart was beating rapidly. Branches scratched her face and grabbed at her clothes. But she didn't care. She needed to get back to Pam and the ponies as fast as she could. She didn't want Tommy and Mike to find the Pony Pals spying on them.

But Pam and the ponies weren't on the trail.

"Where did she go?" whispered Anna in alarm. "Where are the ponies?"

A pony's nicker answered her.

Anna thought she saw the flicker of Snow White's tail inside a large clump of bushes. "Psst. Over here," said Pam.

Anna and Lulu ran over to the bushes. Pam and the three ponies were there. Anna and Lulu squeezed in beside them.

"We found a hideout," Lulu whispered to Pam.

"It's Tommy's and Mike's," added Anna.

"Did you see them?" asked Lulu. "Is that why you warned us?"

"I didn't see them," said Pam, "but I heard them coming along the trail. We hid." She patted Lightning's neck. "Our ponies were so good. They didn't make a sound until they heard Anna's voice. I don't think Tommy and Mike saw us."

"They must have heard you blow the whistle," said Lulu.

"They were kidding around and talking so loud," said Pam, "I don't think they noticed."

"They'd probably think it was birds,

anyway," said Lulu. "They're not very smart about nature."

"Let's go back to our hideout," suggested Anna, "before they find us."

The girls were very quiet all the way back to Pony Pal Lodge. They didn't see or hear Mike and Tommy. When they finally reached the hideout they hitched up their ponies and went inside to have a Pony Pal Meeting.

They sat on the carpet of pine needles and leaned against the mossy rock wall. Lulu passed around cans of juice.

"Mike's and Tommy's hideout is a big mess," Anna told Pam.

"They had a fire in there," added Lulu. "We saw sneaker prints in the ashes."

"I hate that they're hanging out around here," said Anna. "What if they discover our hideout? They'll drive us crazy."

"We have to get them to stop making fires," said Pam.

"How?" asked Anna. "They'll never listen to us."

"We've got a problem," said Lulu.

"A Pony Pal Problem," the three girls said together.

They laughed because they'd all said the same thing at the same instant. But inside, Anna was worried. How could they get Tommy and Mike to stop lighting dangerous fires in the woods?

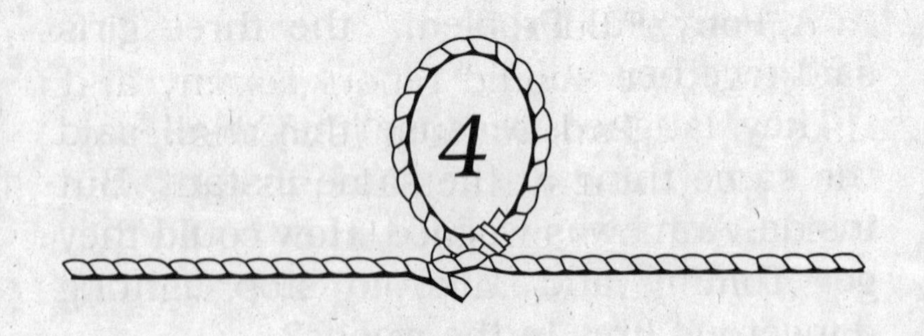

A Warning

"Let's each of us come up with an idea to make Tommy and Mike stop lighting fires in the woods," suggested Lulu.

The three girls were silent for a minute while they thought about it.

Finally, Pam spoke. "You go first, Anna," she said.

"I think we should scare them," said Anna.

"Us scare Tommy and Mike!" exclaimed Pam. "How are we going to do that?"

"I haven't figured out that part yet," admitted Anna.

"What do you think we should do, Pam?" asked Lulu.

"I think we should report Tommy and Mike to the Park Ranger," she answered. "He'll give them a ticket. There's a big fine for lighting fires on state land."

"If they have to pay a fine they'd really learn a lesson," said Anna.

"But Mike's mother doesn't have much money," said Lulu. "It would be hard on her if we report them. I think we should give Tommy and Mike a warning. If that doesn't work then we can report them."

"A warning from us is useless," said Pam. "They'd laugh in our faces."

"We could write them a letter," said Lulu. "And not say it's from us."

"That's good," said Pam. "Let's make it sound like it's from an adult. That might scare them."

"Great idea," agreed Anna. She took out her pad and handed it to Pam. "You write it. You have the best handwriting."

Lulu and Anna moved closer to Pam

and the three girls worked together on a scrap copy of the letter. When they finished, Pam copied it over in her neatest printing.

Boys:

It is illegal to light fires in Morristown.

Also, you have left litter on the trails.

Respect these woods or you will be reported to the Park Ranger. I use these woods, too. I know who you are. I know your parents, Thomas Rand.

And I know your mother, Michael Lacey.

I repeat, RESPECT THESE WOODS.

Also, respect the other people who come here.

This is your one and only warning.

Sincerely Yours,

A Person Who Is Watching You!!!

P.S.

Your hideout is a mess.

"That's a perfect letter," said Anna.

"Let's take it over to their hideout right now."

"They might not be going back there today," said Lulu.

"I want them to read it right away," insisted Pam.

"We could put it under Mike Lacey's door," suggested Anna. "He lives right across the street from my house."

"Anna and I could do it as soon as we get home," added Lulu. "Secretly. We'll sneak in the building and slip it under his door."

"Perfect," said Pam. "It's time to go back, anyway."

The girls went outside and saddled up their ponies. Soon they were riding back to Pam's. Lulu and Anna said their goodbyes to Pam and rode home along Pony Pal Trail.

Back home, Lulu watered and fed Snow White and Acorn. Anna went inside to find an envelope for the letter. She folded the letter, stuck it inside the envelope and sealed it.

Then they went to the picnic table in the Harleys' backyard to review their plan for delivering the letter. Lulu printed "Mike Lacey and Tommy Rand" on the envelope.

"You go into the building," said Lulu. "The Laceys' apartment is at the top of the first set of stairs. Don't let anyone see you. Slip the letter under the door and run down the stairs fast. I'll wait for you behind the building."

The two girls crossed the Town Green. Lulu went behind the apartment building to wait while Anna went inside. Anna climbed the stairs to the second floor and tiptoed over to the Laceys' apartment. She could hear Mrs. Lacey talking on the other side of the door. "I know Tommy has a bigger allowance than you," she was saying. "But I can't afford to give you another penny, Mike. Do you understand?"

"Yes, Ma'am," answered Mike.

Anna was glad that they hadn't reported Mike and Tommy to the Park Ranger yet. She liked Mike's mother and his six-year-old sister, Rosalie. Sometimes she even liked Mike. She wished he would stop hanging around with Tommy Rand. She had a feeling that Mike was nicer when he wasn't with Tommy.

"The light on my bike is busted," Anna heard Mike tell his mother. "I need a new one."

"Take this," said Mrs. Lacey. "But bring me back the change. Get the cheapest one. And don't buy anything else. No candy bars. Do you understand?"

"Yes, Ma'am," answered Mike.

Anna could hear Mike's footsteps approaching the door. Quickly she dropped the letter on the floor in front of the door and raced down the stairs, two at a time. Lulu was waiting for her behind the building.

"Mike's coming out," she told Lulu.

Lulu pointed to the bike rack. "His bike

is here," she said. "What if he comes for it?"

Anna ran towards the trash bins. "Hide!" she ordered.

The two girls ducked behind the trash bins. Anna heard someone coming towards them. She heard the clanking of a bike coming out of a bike rack. Anna counted to twenty before she dared stand up. Mike's bike was gone.

"That was a close call," said Lulu.

"We can go over to the library from here," said Anna. "And come around the other side of the building. It'll look like we were at the library."

Anna stood at the bike rack and looked in the direction of the trash cans. She could see behind them easily. Had Mike seen them?

"Mike could have seen us," she told Lulu.

"Then he might come back," said Lulu with alarm. "Let's go!"

The two girls rushed through the woods to the back of the library building.

"Do you really think Mike knows we're the ones who left that note?" asked Lulu nervously.

"I don't know," admitted Anna.

"I wonder what he and Tommy will do if they figure it out," said Lulu.

Anna wondered about that, too.

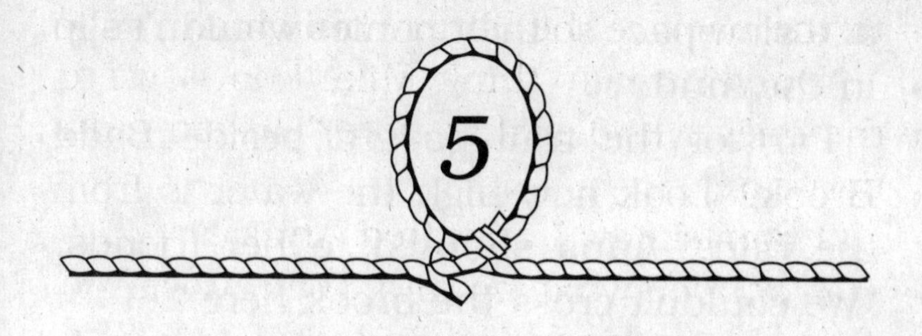

We Were Here

The next morning Anna awoke to the sound of rain pounding on the roof of her house. She looked out the window. The sky was dark gray. She could barely see the pony shelter through the downpour. Well, we won't be going to Pony Pal Lodge today, she thought. And Tommy and Mike won't be lighting any fires, either.

The day after that was still cloudy, but the rain had stopped. Anna met Lulu in the paddock and they rode over to Pam's. Soon the three friends were on the muddy trails that led to Pony Pal Lodge. They rode at a slow pace so their ponies wouldn't slip in the mud.

Part of the trail passed beside Badd Brook. "Look how high the water is from the rain," Anna shouted to her friends. "We couldn't cross the brook here."

"I've never seen it this high," said Pam.

"I'm glad we don't have to go across it to get to Pony Pal Lodge," added Lulu.

Anna wondered if their hideout would be all muddy. She was glad they'd brought their rain gear to sit on. She and Acorn led the way over the narrow trail that ended at their hideout. Anna was the first one to see their rocky enclosure. Something was different. It took her a second to realize what it was. A narrow stream of smoke was rising above their hideout.

"Pam, Lulu, quick!" she shouted. "Our hideout is on fire."

The girls galloped up to the hitching

post. They jumped off their ponies and quickly tied them.

"The water bottles!" shouted Pam. They pulled their water bottles out of their saddle bags and ran into Pony Pal Lodge.

A small fire was smoldering in the middle of the hideout. Pam sprinkled her water over the embers. "Let's not use up all of our water," advised Pam. "The fire's almost out."

Lulu brushed the dry pine needles away with her hands. Anna scraped up some damp dirt and threw it on a charred log.

"Those creeps found our hideout," said Lulu. "Look what they did to Anna's drawings."

Anna looked around. Her two drawings were on the floor. She went over to pick them up. She held up one of the drawings. "Look. There's something written on the back of this one."

Lulu came over and read the note aloud.

PONY PESTS.
MIND YOUR OWN BUSINESS
IF YOU KNOW WHAT'S GOOD FOR YOU.
IT'S A FREE COUNTRY. WE WERE HERE
FIRST. GO AWAY. FIND ANOTHER
PLACE TO PLAY WITH YOUR
LITTLE PONIES.
OR ELSE.

"How dare they threaten us!" shouted Anna. "Those creeps!"

"We'll show them," said Pam. "Let's go over to the Ranger's station right now and report them."

"They deserve it," said Lulu. "This is the last straw."

"We'll have to cross Badd Brook," said Pam. "It's running fast and deep from the rain."

"We can still cross it on our ponies," said Anna. "We'll swim them across."

The three girls ran outside. Anna couldn't wait to report Tommy and Mike to the Park Ranger. She hoped he would give them a huge fine and tell them they could never come back to the Morristown woods. The Ranger's station was on Mt. Morris. One Pony Pal would have to stay at the foot of the mountain with the ponies while the other two climbed up to the station.

"They're gone!" Anna heard Lulu shout. "Our ponies. They're gone!"

Anna looked at the lonely hitching post. Acorn, Snow White and Lightning were nowhere to be seen!

"We hitched them up fast because of the fire," said Anna. "Maybe they got loose. Maybe they ran away."

"Why would our ponies run away?" asked Pam. "They've never done it before. Not when they were all together."

"I bet Tommy and Mike took them," said Anna. "I bet they were spying on us the whole time."

"As soon as we went inside they took our ponies," concluded Pam.

"Why?" asked Lulu. "Why would they take our ponies?"

"They're trying to get back at us for writing that note," said Anna.

"What do they know about ponies?" said Lulu. "What if they try to ride them?"

"Tommy used to ride . . . when he owned Acorn," said Anna.

"That was a long time ago," said Pam. "And I don't think Mike Lacey has ever been on a horse."

"They're such jerks," said Anna. "They could hurt a pony without even trying."

"We've got to find them," said Pam. "And fast."

Suddenly a shock of thunder ripped through the sky. Raindrops fell on Anna's head.

The three girls looked up. The sky was dark with rain clouds. "Let's get our rain gear," said Lulu.

They ran towards their lodge. "Bring

your binoculars and the flashlight," Pam called to Lulu.

"Okay," replied Lulu. "Does anyone have their Pony Pal whistle? Mine is in my saddle bag."

"So is mine," said Pam.

Anna grabbed her raincoat with one hand as she patted her jeans pocket with the other. Her whistle was there. "I've got mine," she said.

In a few minutes the girls were following their ponies' tracks through the woods. They were all running so fast they were breathless. "We have to hurry," Lulu reminded them. "Before the tracks get washed away in the rain."

"And one of the ponies gets hurt," added Pam.

Rainwater streamed down Anna's face. She pulled the hood of her slicker forward. "Acorn, I'll get you away from those dumb boys," she said to herself.

Disappearing Tracks

The Pony Pals followed their ponies' tracks through the woods. The tracks were becoming fainter and fainter in the pouring rain.

Lulu hunched over as she walked now. She was looking for more tracks. When they'd gone a little farther, Lulu stood up and faced Anna and Pam. "There aren't any more tracks to follow," she told them. "The rain has washed them all away."

The three girls huddled together under a tree. Anna looked around. The rain was falling so hard that she could barely see where they were.

"A pony could slip in this mud and break a leg," she told Lulu.

"Snow White is afraid of storms," said Lulu. "She might try to run away."

"What if they let our ponies loose," Pam wondered out loud. "Ponies could panic and get lost in a storm like this."

"Do you think Tommy and Mike went to their hideout?" asked Anna. "To get out of the rain?"

"Maybe," said Pam.

"Then they'd have to cross Badd Brook," Lulu pointed out.

"Which is another dangerous thing to do with ponies," said Pam, "if you don't ride them across."

"Tommy and Mike would never know that," said Lulu.

"I bet they've gone to their hideout to get out of the rain," said Anna.

"Let's check it out," agreed Lulu.

"Come on," said Pam. "I know a place

on the brook that shouldn't be too hard to cross."

Lulu and Anna followed Pam through the woods.

Anna thought, what if Tommy or Mike try to ride Acorn on slippery ground? What if they hit him to try to make him do what they want? Tears mixed with the rain streaming down Anna's face.

Pam led the way to a spot on Badd Brook where the girls could jump across from rock to rock. When they were on the other side they walked along a deer run beside the swollen brook. The rain was finally slowing down.

Anna had never seen the water in Badd Brook so high. She remembered all the fun times she'd had in the brook with Acorn. She thought she heard him whinny.

Lulu grabbed Anna's arm and put out a hand to stop Pam. "Listen," she told them. She had heard the whinny, too.

The Pony Pals stayed perfectly still and

listened. They all heard a whinny. This time it was louder.

"They're on the other side of the brook," said Pam. "They didn't cross it after all."

Anna looked across the brook. "I think I see Tommy's red jacket," she said. "They're coming in this direction."

"Quick! Hide!" ordered Lulu. "Don't let them see us."

The three girls scooted behind a stand of pine trees. Lulu looked through the binoculars. "I see them!" she exclaimed.

Lulu handed the binoculars to Anna.

Anna held them up and looked through. She moved her head until she saw a hand holding reins. Tommy was holding onto Snow White. She looked to the right. Mike was holding Lightning's lead rope. Where was Acorn? Anna twisted around until she saw Acorn on the other side of Lightning. No one was holding onto him. Acorn sniffed and looked around. He wonders where I am, thought Anna. He would come if I called him. "All the ponies are there," Anna told Lulu and Pam. She handed the binoculars to Pam.

Pam looked through them. "Tommy and Mike are staring at the brook like they don't know what to do," Pam observed.

"What are we going to do?" asked Lulu. "How can we get our ponies away from them when there is a brook between us?"

"If I blow my whistle maybe Acorn will come across the brook to reach me," Anna told Lulu and Pam.

"Then Tommy and Mike will know we found them," said Pam. "They'll run away with Lightning and Snow White. And we'll only have one pony."

"Good point," agreed Anna.

"I have an idea," said Lulu. "Let's go back to where we can cross the brook on rocks. Then we'll sneak up behind Tommy and Mike. We'll ambush them and get back our ponies."

"What if they leave while we're trying to get there," said Pam.

"I'll stay here to keep an eye on them,"

said Anna. "If I think they're trying to go anywhere I'll let them know I'm here. I'll pretend I'm really upset and let them tease me. They won't leave if they think they're upsetting me. It's their idea of fun."

"You don't mind?" asked Lulu.

"Not if it helps get our ponies back," said Anna.

Pam handed Anna the binoculars. "Use these for spying on them," she said.

Pam and Lulu left, and Anna was alone. She leant against a tree and looked through the binoculars. First she found Acorn. He was still near Lightning. Next she focused on Tommy's face. He didn't have on a rain jacket and was sopping wet. He looked worried. He said something to Mike and pointed to his right, as if he was saying, "That's the way we should go."

Anna turned a little and focused on Mike. He shook his head and pointed to the left. Mike looked worried, too. Tommy and Mike are lost, thought Anna. They don't know which way to go. And they're afraid to cross Badd Brook. Will they leave? Anna wondered. Can I keep them there while Pam and Lulu cross the brook and sneak up on them?

7

Lost!

Anna kept spying on Tommy, Mike and the stolen ponies through the binoculars. She figured that it would take Pam and Lulu at least ten minutes to reach them.

During the next few minutes the boys continued to argue about which way to go. Finally, Mike nodded. He was agreeing to go the way Tommy was pointing. They were going to leave with the ponies.

Anna had to act fast or the Pony Pals would lose their chance to rescue their ponies. She left her hiding place and ran towards the brook. I have to be a terrific actor, thought Anna. She had to keep Tommy and Mike there. She had to let them tease her.

When Anna reached the edge of the brook she shouted, "Give me back my pony! Please."

Acorn whinnied when he heard Anna's voice.

Anna watched Mike and Tommy through the binoculars. Tommy said something to Mike and the two boys started laughing.

"Hey, Pony Pest," Tommy called. "We can't hear you!"

"Give me back my pony!" shouted Anna.

"Give me back my pony," Tommy shouted back.

"I mean it, Tommy Rand," yelled Anna. "You have to give us back our ponies. Or we'll have you arrested."

"I mean it, Tommy Rand," repeated Mike. "You have to give us back our ponies. Or we'll have you arrested."

"Oh, oh," said Tommy in a silly, high-pitched voice. "I'm so scared."

"Please," Anna shouted across the brook. "Please, give me back my pony."

"Please. Please, give me back my pony," repeated Tommy and Mike together.

She wished that Lulu and Pam would hurry up and get there so she could stop this performance. She wiped pretend tears from her cheeks with her hand. "We'll do anything to get our ponies back," she cried.

"Then stay away from our hideout!" yelled Mike.

"I'm sorry I went into your hideout," Anna shouted back. "We'll never do it again."

"And stay out of the woods," added Tommy.

I'd like to scream at those guys, thought Anna. The woods don't belong to them. They almost destroyed the forest with their fires. I'll tell them what I really think later. But now I have to distract them.

"Okay," she told Tommy and Mike. "We won't ride here anymore. Can I have my pony back now?"

"Come and get him," said Tommy with a laugh.

"You know I can't cross the brook here," she said. "You ride him over."

Tommy and Mike just laughed. Anna looked at her watch. Pam and Lulu would be there very soon. It would be easier for them to rescue the ponies if they only had to get two. She raised her whistle to her lips and let out one big blast. Then she yelled, "Acorn, come."

Before Tommy and Mike knew what happened, Acorn broke away from them and ran along the side of the brook. "Hey, come back here!" Tommy screamed. He and Mike chased after Acorn.

Anna blew her whistle again. Acorn whinnied at Anna as if to say, "Here I come," and plunged into the water. He waded through the fast-moving current towards Anna. She cheered him on. When

Acorn reached the other side, he hopped up the bank and ran right over to Anna. He shook his wet mane at her and nickered as if to say, "Why did you let those stupid boys keep me so long?"

Tommy and Mike stood by the side of the brook with their hands on their hips.

"We still have two ponies!" shouted Mike.

"And we won't let them go," added Tommy.

Anna now saw Lulu and Pam come out of the woods behind the boys. The boys turned around to go back to Snow White and Lightning. But Pam and Lulu reached their ponies first and swung up on them.

Tommy and Mike were completely surprised by the Pony Pal ambush. Before they knew what had happened, the girls were riding their ponies into the brook.

Anna and Acorn met their Pony Pals at the brook's edge. The girls hooted and cheered as Pam and Lulu jumped down

from Lightning and Snow White. The three girls hugged.

"Tommy and Mike don't know how to get out of the woods," Anna quickly whispered to Lulu and Pam. "They're lost."

"Great," said Lulu.

"Let's just leave them here," said Anna. "That's what they deserve."

"Hey, Pam!" shouted Tommy. "We didn't hurt your ponies. It was just a joke."

"Some joke!" Pam yelled back. "They could have been hurt or lost."

"Just like you," added Anna.

"Lost!" exclaimed Mike. "We're not lost. It's just this stupid brook has too much water in it."

"They don't know they can get home from that side of the brook," Anna whispered. "They don't know about the secret trail."

"Should we tell them?" Pam asked.

"No!" said Anna and Lulu in unison.

"We can tell them a safe place to cross

the brook," said Lulu. "Then they can get back along the Morristown Trail."

"But only after we're sure they won't bother us or our ponies again," added Pam. "If they won't promise and still act like jerks, we should turn them in."

How are we going to do that? wondered Anna.

They had to come up with a Pony Pal Plan. And fast.

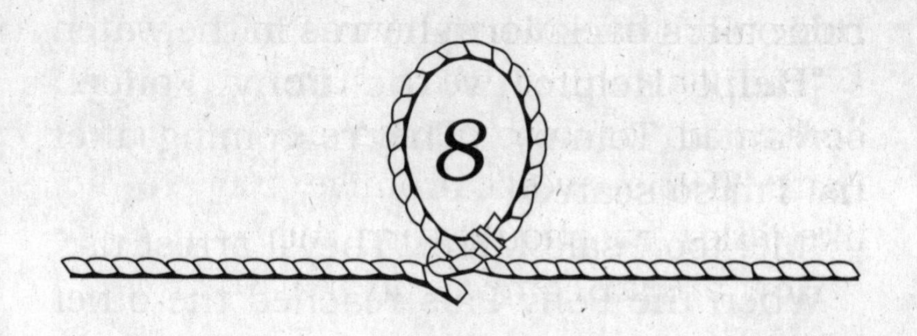

8

Afraid

"Let's ride back to their side of the brook," said Pam.

"And stay on our ponies so we're taller than they are," suggested Anna.

The girls mounted their ponies. Acorn's saddle was wet from the rain, but she didn't care. She was happy to have her pony back.

Pam led the way into the brook on Lightning. Lulu and Snow White followed. Anna didn't have to urge Acorn to follow Snow White and Lightning into the brook.

Acorn loved the water. And Anna loved to ride on his back when he was in the water.

"Help! Help! It's the Pony Police!" screamed Tommy. "They're coming after us. I'm so scared!"

"Me, too," said Mike. "They'll arrest us."

When the Pony Pals reached the other side of the brook they didn't dismount. They rode right up to the boys. Anna liked looking down on them. Acorn shook his mane in Tommy's face.

"Hey!" shouted Tommy.

Anna laughed as she backed up Acorn.

"Taking our ponies was really stupid!" said Lulu.

"And dangerous," added Pam.

Anna moved Acorn close to Tommy again. "Our ponies could have been hurt," she said angrily.

"We weren't going to hurt your little ponies," said Tommy.

"Maybe not on purpose," said Lulu. "But it still could have happened."

"You went into our clubhouse," said Mike.

"We don't like little kids messing with our stuff," added Tommy. "Got the message?"

Lightning nudged Mike. He backed away. Anna thought that Mike was a little afraid of Lightning.

"We went into your messy clubhouse because we saw smoke," Anna told the boys. "We saved your stupid clubhouse."

"And the woods," added Lulu.

"Don't you guys know that campfires aren't allowed in the State Parks," said Pam. "It's the law."

"You said it was okay to have a fire," Anna heard Mike whisper to Tommy.

"It's a stupid law," argued Tommy.

Mike put his hands in his pockets and backed farther away from Lightning. "We didn't burn any trees down or anything," he mumbled.

"That's because we put those fires out,"

said Lulu. "You've got to stop making fires."

"Or we'll report you to the Park Ranger," said Anna.

"We *are* reporting you to the Park Ranger," added Pam. "I've had it with you, Tommy Rand. You are totally irresponsible."

Mike shifted nervously from foot to foot. He's really scared, thought Anna. Mike knows that if we tell the Park Ranger, the Ranger will talk to his mother, and he'll be in big trouble. "Hey, don't turn us in," he pleaded. "We were just fooling around. That note. Taking your ponies. It was all a joke. Right, Tommy?"

Tommy ignored Mike. "I don't care. I'm not afraid of the Park Ranger," he said.

"Okay," said Pam. "I'll go see the Park Ranger."

She turned Lightning around and rode away.

Anna and Lulu exchanged a glance. Anna didn't mind getting Tommy Rand in trouble. She wasn't so sure she wanted to get Mike in trouble. She thought Lulu felt the same way. But the Pony Pals had to be united in front of Mike and Tommy. Lulu turned Snow White around and followed Pam. Anna and Acorn took up the rear.

"Hey," shouted Mike. "How do we get out of here? We can't get across the brook."

"Shut up," Anna heard Tommy tell Mike.

But it was too late. The Pony Pals knew for sure that Mike and Tommy were lost.

Anna and Lulu followed Pam onto the trail that led to Mt. Morris and the Park Ranger's station. "Wait up," Anna called.

But Pam didn't stop until she reached the narrow footpath that led up the mountain. By the time Lulu and Anna pulled up, Pam was dismounting.

"I'm climbing the mountain to the Ranger's station," she said. "Who's staying with the ponies and who's coming with me?"

"Pam, wait," said Lulu. "We have to talk about this."

"I don't care what you two think," Pam told Anna and Lulu. "I'm reporting those guys." Pam's eyes were flashing. Anna had never seen her so mad.

"Pam," said Lulu. "This is a Pony Pal Problem. At least two people have to agree on what to do."

"I think we should give them another chance," said Anna.

"Me, too," said Lulu.

Pam turned and ran up the path. Anna ran after her. She grabbed Pam's hand. "Please, wait," she pleaded. "It will take you at least an hour to climb up there. Then you have to come back. He's probably not even there. We can report them later."

Pam looked at the steep trail ahead of her and then at Anna. "You're right," she said. "He's probably not there."

Anna and Pam walked back to Lulu and the ponies.

"Lightning looks tired," said Lulu. "I think we should give our ponies a rest."

Lightning gave a little nicker as if to say, "I *am* tired. Please take care of me."

"I'm just so angry at those two, especially Tommy," said Pam. "He doesn't respect anything."

"We're angry, too," said Lulu. "But let's just slow down here and take care of our ponies. Okay?"

Pam rubbed her hand along Lightning's sweaty neck. "Okay," agreed Pam. "Besides, the Ranger might come by here. It's the only trail to the station."

Anna felt the water sloshing around in her wet boots. Acorn's mane was matted. Pam's raincoat was half off her shoulders and her hair was dripping wet. Lightning was still breathing hard from the ride. Lulu's jeans were muddy and Snow White didn't look like a white pony anymore.

"Look at us," giggled Anna. "We're a mess."

Pam and Lulu laughed, too.

"Let's clean up," said Pam.

The girls removed saddles and bridles and hung them over the hitching post to dry. Steam rose off the wet ponies.

It had turned into a sunny, warm day. The girls took off their rain jackets and wet shoes and socks and put those out to dry, too.

"Guess what I just remembered?" Anna said excitedly. "We have our lunches with us. We never unpacked them."

"All right!" shouted Pam and Lulu.

The girls sat on a rock in the sun to dry off and have a picnic. Their ponies slept. Anna hoped the Park Ranger wouldn't come by. She wanted to have a Pony Pal Meeting about what to do with Tommy and Mike.

The Red Jacket

"I want to report Tommy and Mike to the Park Ranger for lighting fires," Pam told Anna and Lulu. "Then we'll go to the State Police and report that they stole our ponies."

Anna swallowed a bite of her sandwich. "Mike didn't know there was a law against campfires," she said. "I don't think he'd make another one."

"Maybe he wouldn't," said Pam. "But Tommy would. If he wants to do something, he just does it. He doesn't care about any rules. When we were little he was always breaking rules."

"Did you really used to play with him?" asked Lulu.

"A lot," answered Pam. "His mother and my mother were friends. They thought it was so cute that Tommy and I played together. But Tommy was always getting me into trouble."

The Pony Pals looked at one another and thought for a second. Now that she'd calmed down, Anna could think clearly. If someone was lost in the woods—even someone she didn't like—she had to help them. She knew that Pam and Lulu were thinking the same thing.

"We better go help them," said Pam. "We can talk about whether to report them to the Park Ranger later."

The three girls put on their socks and shoes and saddled up their ponies. It was time to rescue Tommy and Mike.

Pam pulled down Lightning's stirrups

and mounted. "Let's go," she said. "We have to find them before it gets dark."

The Pony Pals rode onto the trail that led to Badd Brook. Anna led the way. They hadn't gone very far when she saw a flash of red through the trees to her left. Was it a bird? She slowed down and looked more closely. It was Mike's red jacket. Anna halted and turned in the saddle to signal Pam and Lulu to stop.

"They're in the woods," she whispered. "Should we spy on them before we tell them how to get home?"

"Absolutely," answered Lulu.

"I'll stay with the ponies," offered Pam.

Anna and Lulu crept through the woods towards the flash of red. When they came closer, Anna saw that Tommy was sitting on an old log and Mike was pacing up and down in front of him. Anna and Lulu hid behind trees to listen.

"You didn't tell me we could get in trouble for lighting fires," Mike was

saying. "My mother would kill me if she found out."

"Who would want to come back to these stupid woods again anyway?" said Tommy. "I hate it here."

"We're going to be out here all night," said Mike. "My clothes are still wet. We'll probably freeze to death."

"If we're lost it's your fault," grumbled Tommy. "You were too afraid to cross the brook. Now we can't even find the stupid brook."

Anna motioned to Lulu and they sneaked back to Pam.

Acorn whinnied when he saw Anna. She wondered if Tommy and Mike heard him.

"They are totally lost," Lulu told Pam.

"Don't make it easy for them," said Anna.

"And if they act like jerks again, we'll lead them in the wrong direction," suggested Pam.

"We'll pretend that's the way home,"

added Lulu. "We won't tell them unless they stop being jerks."

"Shush," warned Pam. "Here they come."

Tommy and Mike pushed their way through the bushes and came out on the trail.

"Hey," said Tommy. "Look who's here. It's the Pony Pests."

"You guys on your way home?" asked Mike.

"We're not going home yet," Lulu told the boys. "We like it in the woods. Don't you?"

"Yeah, sure," said Tommy. "But we're going home now."

"Really?" said Pam. "Which way are you going?"

Tommy pointed in one direction and Mike pointed in the other. Neither of them was correct. Anna pretended to cough so the boys wouldn't see her laugh.

"We have to cross Badd Brook," said Mike. "But it's pretty deep right now."

They really don't know about the secret trail, thought Anna. They think the only way to go home is to cross the brook and go on the Morristown Trail.

"We'll tell you how to get back," said Pam. "But you have to promise not to light any more fires."

"A cross-your-heart promise," added Anna.

"A cross-your-heart promise," mimicked Tommy.

Anna felt her face flush with anger. How dare Tommy make fun of her when he needed the Pony Pals' help?

The Pony Pals exchanged a glance. "Let's go home," said Lulu. The three girls mounted their ponies. Pam led the way along the trail.

"See you around," said Anna.

Park Ranger

Tommy and Mike ran behind the Pony Pals and their ponies. "Hey, wait up," Tommy called.

"He was just kidding around," yelled Mike.

"Can't you take a joke?" shouted Tommy.

"Watch out!" Anna shouted back. "Don't get too close. You could get kicked!"

Anna didn't have to worry about Tommy and Mike. They couldn't keep up with the galloping ponies. But she knew they would follow them.

Pam suddenly slowed Lightning to a walk. "Look," she called to Anna and Lulu. "There's the Park Ranger."

Anna looked past Pam and saw Jack Stranton, the Park Ranger, riding towards them on a trail bike.

"Hi, there," Jack called out. He leaned his bike on a tree and came over to talk to the girls.

"I wondered if the Pony Pals were around here today," he said. "I was afraid you were caught in that downpour. That was a sudden one, wasn't it?"

"It sure was," said Anna. "And we were caught in it."

Jack looked more carefully at the girls and their ponies. "You don't look wet," he said.

"We had our rain jackets with us," said Anna. "And we dried the rest of our stuff out in the sun."

"Good for you," Jack said. "You sure know how to get along in the woods." He looked past the Pony Pals. "I see you have some friends with you today."

Anna turned around. Tommy and Mike were catching up to them.

"They're not our friends," she said.

"But we know them," added Lulu.

"They've been driving us a little crazy," said Anna. "Now I think they're lost."

"You should probably tell them how to get back to town," added Pam.

Tommy and Mike stopped when they saw the Park Ranger. They looked like they were going to turn around and run the other way. Jack motioned to them. "You boys. Come on over here," he shouted.

Mike and Tommy walked over to Jack.

"I haven't seen you around here before," he said in a very official voice. "What are your names?" He took out a notepad and pencil.

Mike's voice shook when he told the Park Ranger his name. He's really scared,

thought Anna. Even Tommy looked a little pale.

The Ranger wrote both boys' names on his notepad. "You two wouldn't be responsible for the campfires I've seen in the woods over the past few days, would you?"

"I didn't know it was against the law," Mike blurted out. "I swear."

Tommy glared at the girls. "Tattletales," he mumbled.

"They didn't tell me it was you," said Jack. "And I didn't say it was. I just asked." He smiled at Tommy and Mike. "But now I guess I do know who has been lighting those fires."

Tommy punched Mike in the arm. "You jerk," he said.

Mike winced and jumped back. "Hey, man," he said. "You're always getting me in trouble. So quit it."

Tommy ignored Mike. "It was all his idea," Tommy told the Park Ranger. "I tried to stop him."

The Pony Pals looked at one another. Tommy was putting the blame on someone else—again.

"I'm not interested in whose idea it was. But listen to me carefully," Jack said in a firm voice. "I go through these woods every day. If I see either of you in these woods again—or evidence of campfires—I'm visiting your parents and giving you both a hefty fine to pay. This is your only warning. Do you understand?"

"Yes, sir," said Mike.

"Don't worry," Tommy said. "I'm never coming back here. These woods are stupid."

"I don't think the woods are the problem, young man," said the Park Ranger. "I think your attitude and actions are. Now go home."

"Yes, sir," said Mike.

Tommy started walking up the trail. He was heading in the wrong direction. Mike followed him.

The Ranger watched them for a minute.

He smiled at the Pony Pals. "How far should I let them go before I tell them how to get home?" he asked.

Anna thought Tommy might really learn a lesson if he spent a night in the woods. But she felt sorry for Mike. And she thought he at least had learned a lesson. "It's already a long way back to town," she said.

"And it'll be dark soon," added Pam.

"But please tell them how to get back to the Morristown Trail," said Anna. "We don't want them to know about the trail that starts behind that big rock on Riddle Road."

"No problem," said Jack.

Mike's red jacket was becoming smaller and smaller. But the Park Ranger and the Pony Pals could hear that they were still arguing.

Jack jumped on his bike. "I'd better catch up with them before they kill one another," he said. He rode off.

"We'll be home way before Mike and Tommy," said Lulu.

Anna leaned over and patted Acorn on the neck. "We have great transportation."

"Here they come," Pam announced.

Anna saw Tommy and Mike running along the trail in their direction.

"Hey, wait," yelled Tommy. "That guy said you should lend us a pony to ride home."

"Hey, wait," shouted Anna. "That guy said you should lend us a pony to ride home."

Pam and Lulu laughed.

"Very funny," Tommy shouted. "But seriously, wait up."

"Very funny," the Pony Pals hollered in unison. "But seriously, wait up."

"Let's go," Pam told Anna and Lulu. "They know the way home now."

"I've had enough of those guys," added Anna.

Acorn whinnied as if to say, "Me, too."

The Pony Pals turned their three ponies around and galloped towards home.

Dear Reader:

I am having a lot of fun researching and writing books about the Pony Pals. I've met many interesting kids and adults who love ponies. And I've visited some wonderful ponies at homes, farms, and riding schools.

Before writing Pony Pals I wrote fourteen novels for children and young adults. Four of these were honored by Children's Choice Awards.

I live in Sharon, Connecticut, with my husband, Lee, and our dog, Willie. Our daughter is all grown up and has her own apartment in New York City.

Besides writing novels I like to draw, paint, garden, and swim. I didn't have a pony when I was growing up, but I have always loved them and dreamt about riding. Now I take riding lessons on a horse named Saz.

I like reading and writing about ponies as much as I do riding. Which proves to me that you don't have to ride a pony to love them. And you certainly don't need a pony to be a Pony Pal.

Happy Reading,

Jeanne Betancourt